GRUMPY
PANTS

words & pictures by
CLAIRE MESSER

Albert Whitman & Company
Chicago, Illinois

Penguin was in a bad mood.
A very bad mood.

He didn't know why
and he didn't care.

He stomped his feet
all the way home.

He pulled off his grumpy coat
and kicked off his grumpy boots.

But he was still grumpy.

He tried to shake it off.

But he was still grumpy.

So he pulled off one grumpy sock
and then the other.

But he was still grumpy.

So he took off his grumpy overalls...

Nope. Still grumpy.

Finally, he took off his grumpy underpants.

"I'm still grumpy, you know."

Then penguin took a deep breath
and he counted...

One...

two...

three...

SPL

The water was nice and cold.
Penguin played with his duck.

He hid under the water and made
himself a bubble beard.

Little by little, he was starting to feel much better.

It was time to get out of the tub.

He put on his favorite pajamas.

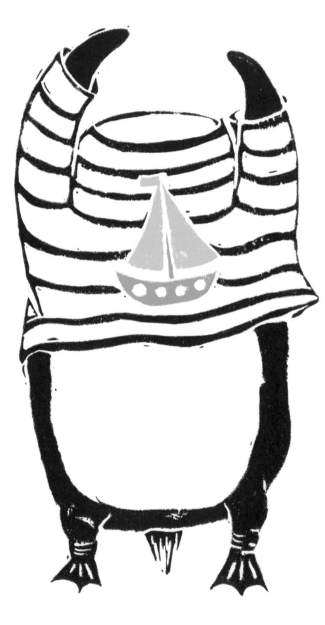

And he had a steaming
cup of hot chocolate.

He read his favorite book.

He found his favorite teddy
and climbed into bed.

As Penguin fell asleep, he knew that tomorrow would be a good day

because all the grumpiness
had been washed away.

For my big sister, Kirsten, and my husband, Simon,
thanks for teaching me all about hissy fits.

Library of Congress Cataloging-in-Publication
data is on file with the publisher.
Text and pictures copyright © 2016 by Claire Messer
Published in 2016 by Albert Whitman & Company
ISBN 978-0-8075-3075-7

Printed in China
10 9 8 7 6 5 4 LP 23 22 21 20 19 18 17 16

Design by Jordan Kost

For more information about Albert Whitman & Company,
visit our web site at www.albertwhitman.com.